I'm the Biggest Thing in the Ocean

I'm bigger than plankton

To my parents, who were always the biggest thing in my ocean

ISBN-13: 978-0-545-10988-8
ISBN-10: 0-545-10988-4

12 11 10 9 8 7 6 5 4 3 2 1   8 9 10 11 12 13/0

Printed in the U.S.A.   08

This edition first printing, September 2008

Designed by Teresa Kietlinski Dikun

Text set in Bookman, Blue Century

The art was completed in three layers, each separated by glass that was pried from the windows of shipwrecked pirate ships. There is a watercolor layer background, then a cut-paper level, and finally, an ink layer consisting of 100% fresh squid ink.

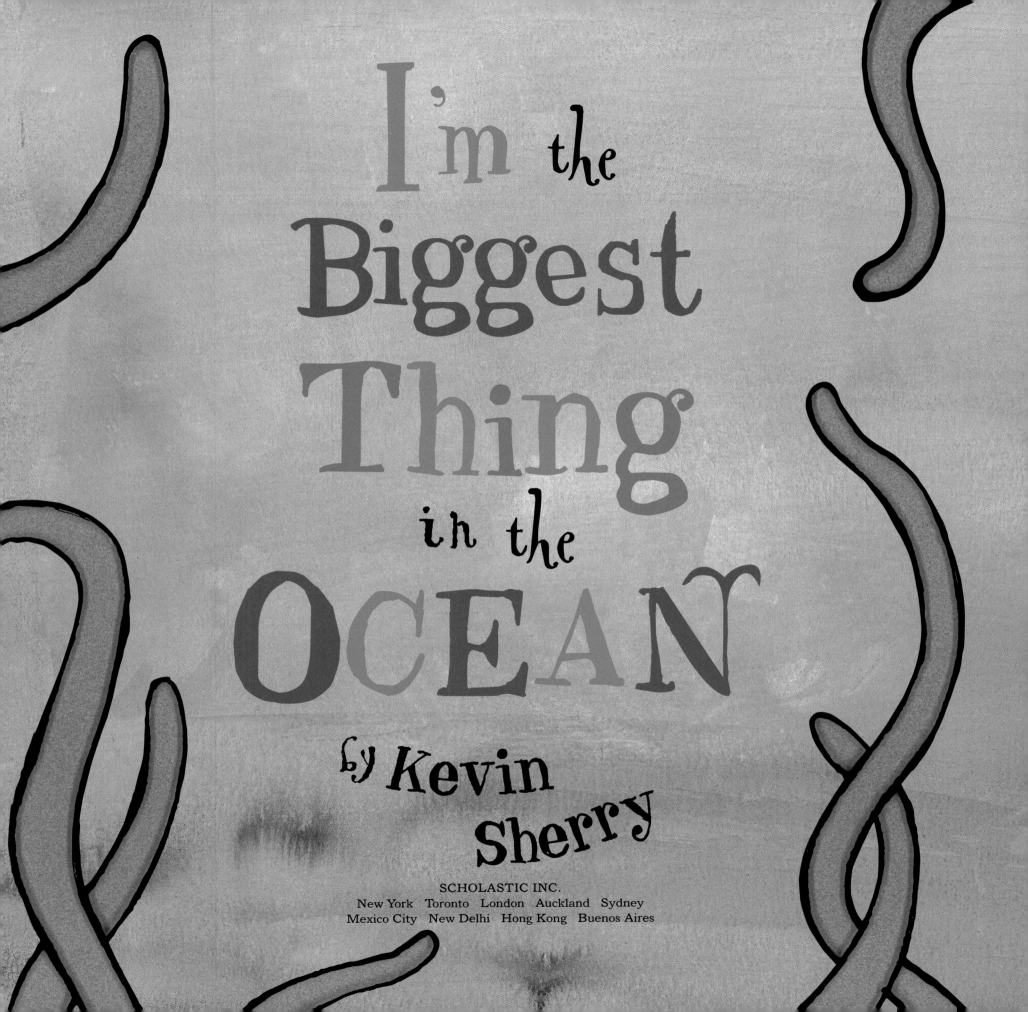

I'm the Biggest Thing in the OCEAN

by Kevin Sherry

SCHOLASTIC INC.
New York   Toronto   London   Auckland   Sydney
Mexico City   New Delhi   Hong Kong   Buenos Aires

I'm a GIANT squid
and I'm BIG.

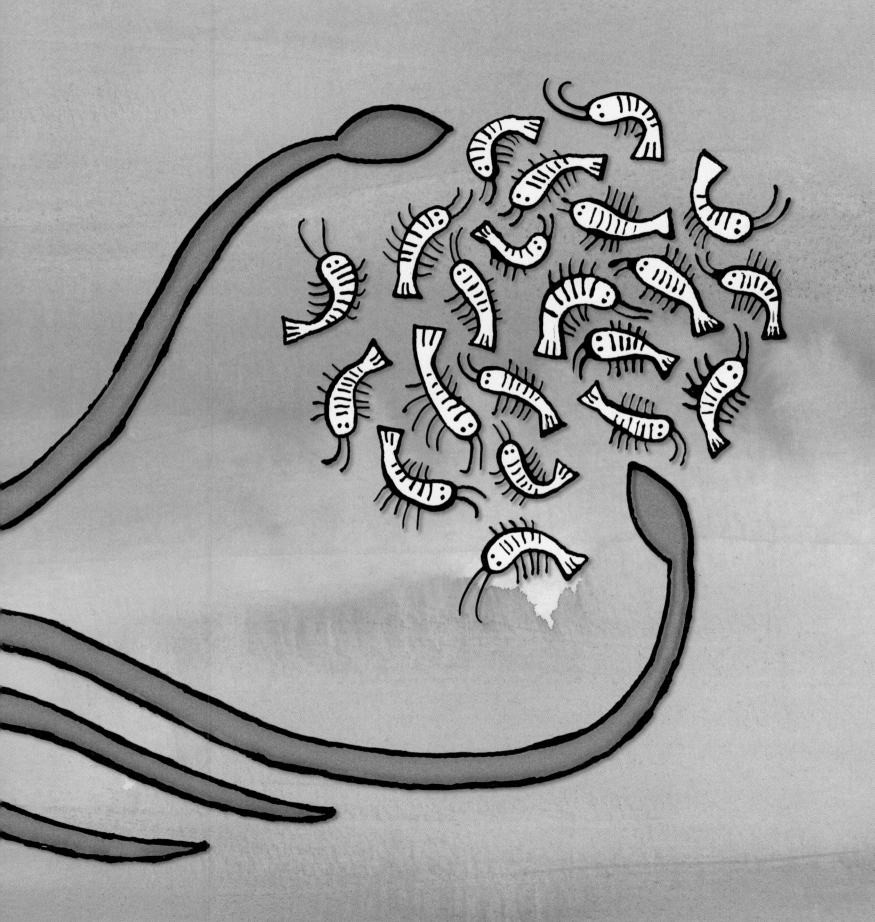

this fish,

and that fish.

that fish,

this fish,

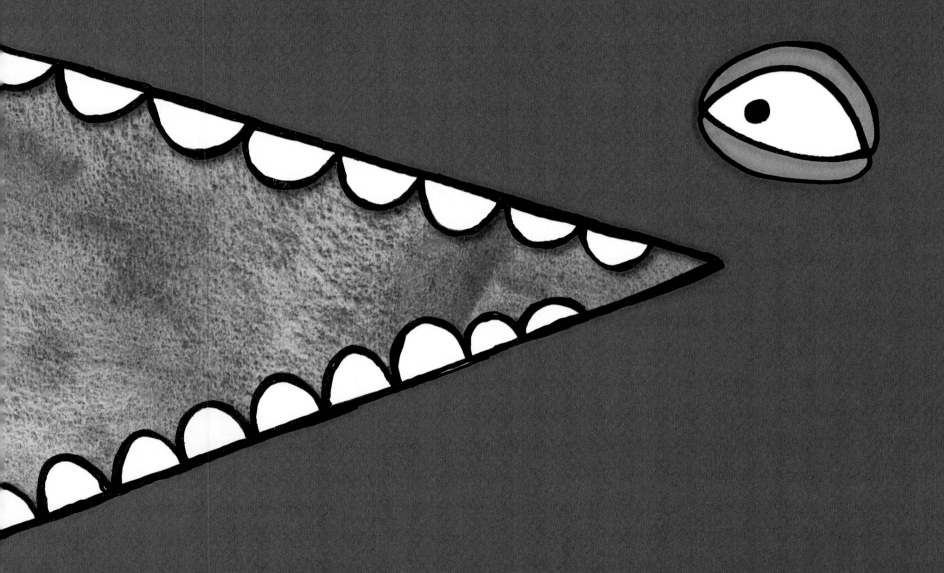

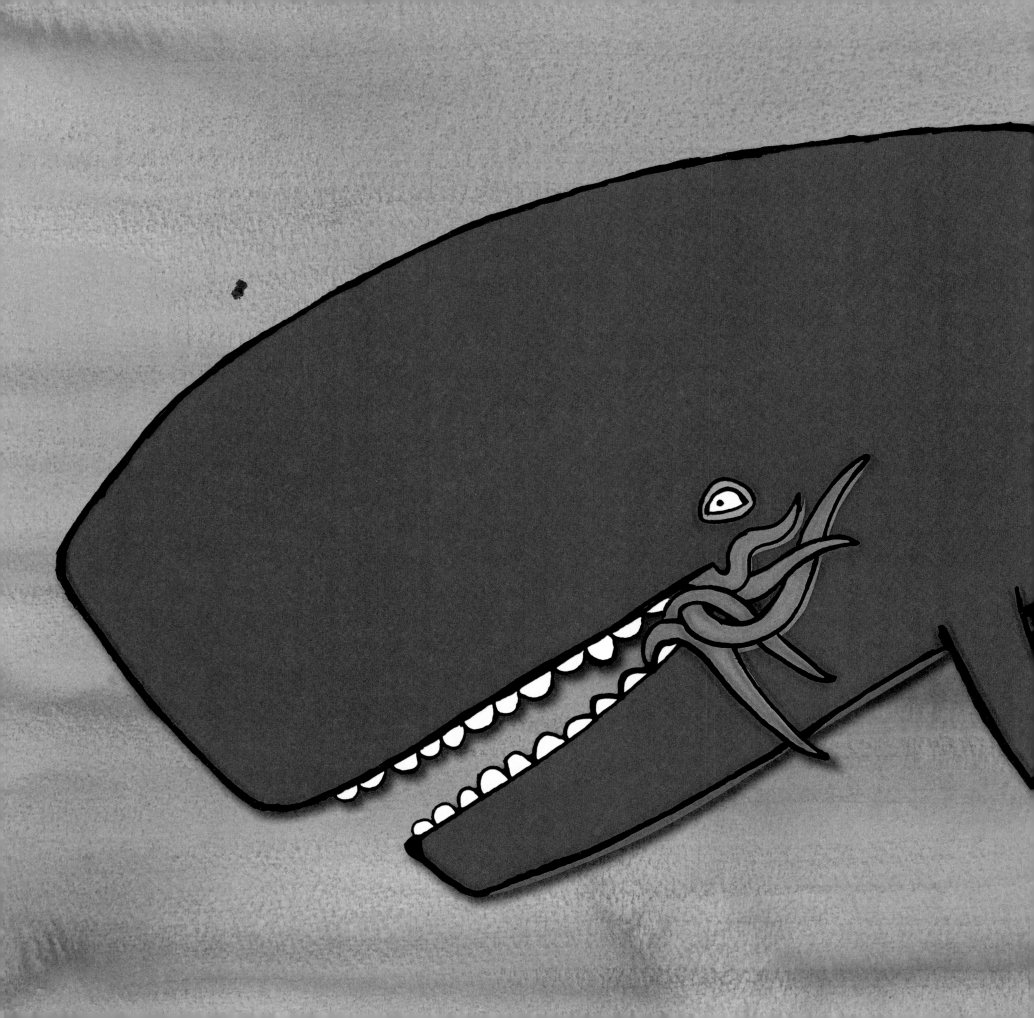

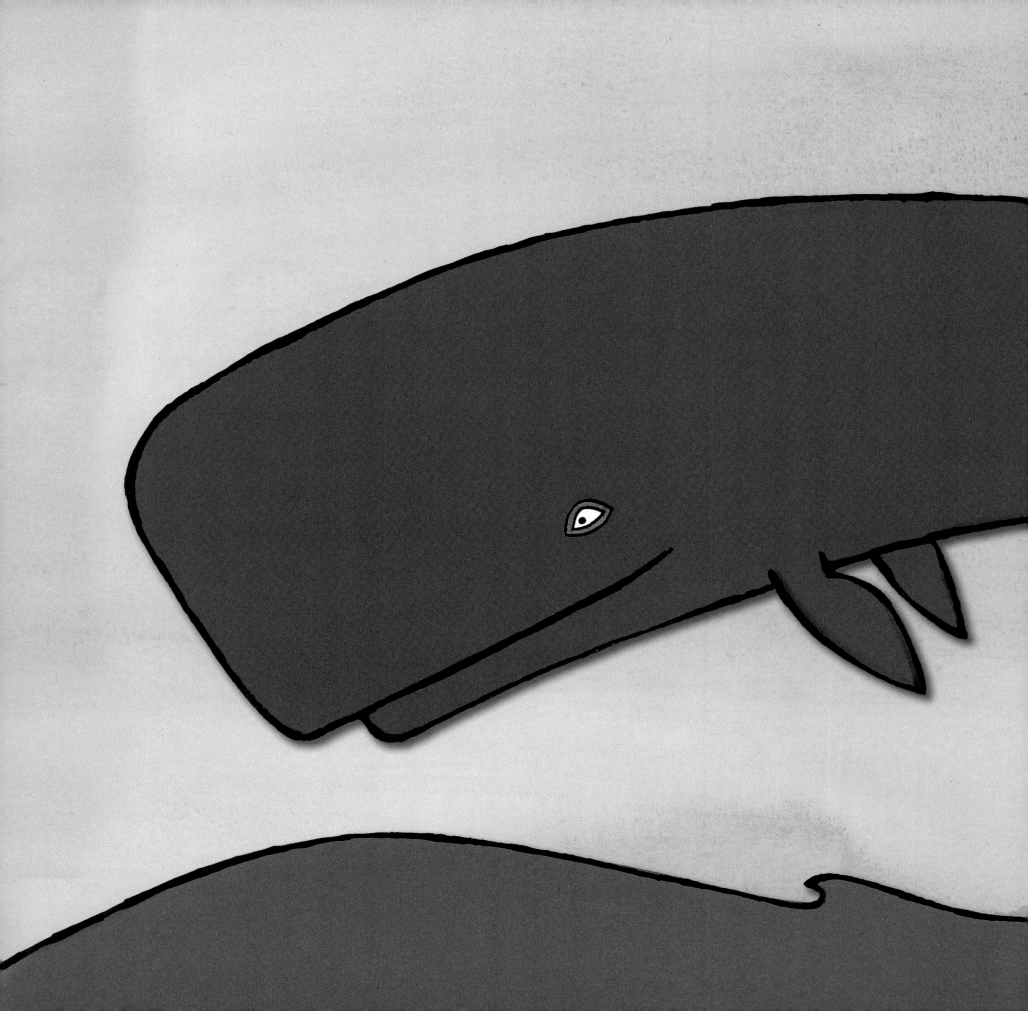